THE GLORY WHOLE PACKAGE

THE CURSED MATCHMAKER
BOOK 1

SABRINA CROSS

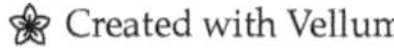 Created with Vellum

AUTHOR'S NOTE

This is a sentient object romance. Humans will be getting it on with sentient objects. Don't worry, everyone is gleefully consenting.

If you read the last three sentences and think that's not for you, that's okay. There is still time to put this book down and walk away. No one will blame you. It's the sane thing to do.

But if you're going to stick around please be aware of the following: use of glory hole, anonymous sex, not-so anonymous sex, dubious consent between consenting adults, oral sex, vaginal sex, anal sex, a man cursed into a glory hole, voyuerism, edging, negative self-talk/shame, disassociation during sex.

If you feel I am missing anything please reach out to me at authorsabrinacross@gmail.com and let me know. A complete list can be found at <u>www.sabrinacross.com</u>

CHAPTER 1
JOSH

She's back.

I tremble with anticipation and excitement as the door closes. The scent of apples fills the air. There's a sharp inhale, and a resigned sigh. Then the sound of clothes rustling as she removes them.

I wish I knew what she looks like. If she drops the clothes to the floor in a pile, ready and excited to get to it, or if she hangs them neatly. Maybe she folds them on the chair with great care. I don't know. I can't tell from sound alone and it kills me.

It is just another part of my punishment. To always be in such close proximity to warm and willing flesh but never allowed to see, to touch, to taste. It is its own kind of Hell.

I bite back a groan as the woman who smells of green apples drops to her knees in front of me. The smell intensifies and I imagine her pulling her hair up or tying it into a braid. Something to get it out of the way as she prepares herself for what comes next.

We both know what comes next and while she's practically vibrating with anticipation, I'm trapped in the dark, anticipating the agony to come.

That's what my life is now. Darkness, pleasure, and pain. Whoever said you couldn't die of blue balls clearly hadn't been magically castrated and fucked to the edge multiple times.

But death isn't in the cards for me. My captor will never allow it. Instead, I remain as I have been for two long years, trapped, immobile, locked in darkness. And, like the woman who smells of green apples, I wait for something I want but know I cannot have.

CHAPTER 2
SAMANTHA

his is the last time," I mutter to myself as I enter the small, dim room. It's a mantra I tell myself every time I do this, but I know I don't mean it.

I flick the lock and begin to strip. It's not a requirement but sometimes things get messy and I'd rather not walk out of there covered in drool. I would hardly be the first person to do it, but it just isn't my style.

Nothing about what I am doing is my typical style. It is insane. Absolutely and utterly insane. But knowing it and being able to stop myself were two totally different things.

I hang my dress on the hook and take a deep breath. I can walk out of there right now. No one would ever be the wiser, except for my best friend, Bethany. She wouldn't judge me for changing my mind. She'd probably be relieved my bout of insanity has passed.

Instead, I cross the small room to drop to my knees before the hole in the wall. I quickly braid my hair away from my face and secure it with the hair tie looped around my wrist. I'd learned the first time not to leave my hair down. Not only is it a magnet for bodily fluids, but it gets in the way. And I want nothing spoiling this for me.

My eyes close and my breathing slows as I listen for the sound of the door on the other side of the thin, black wall. I need this and I need it with him, the man who is about to walk through the door.

I just wish he knew it was me.

CHAPTER 3
HARVEY

This is the very last time I am going to do this. I'm done being reduced to this mess of need. Lust claws at my throat as I enter the small, dimly lit room. The sounds of the club disappear when I close the door.

I don't bother to take off my clothes or even remove my jacket as I cross to the wall. I just undo my belt and pants, sliding them just far enough down to draw my cock out. I'm already half-hard. It's a familiar state. I have been half hard since the moment I hired Samantha to be my assistant. Six achingly long months of erections as she proficiently goes about her business.

She's why I'm there, about to stick my dick into a hole in the wall and let some nameless, faceless woman suck me off.

I rip open the condom wrapper and quickly roll it on. I understand and agree with the need for them, but I long to forego the protection and just feel her mouth on me. Bare. The way I would take Samantha's mouth if I could.

But there are a lot of inherent risks in what I'm doing and I don't want to take more than necessary to get what I need. Being here, doing this, is risky enough.

I don't say anything as I slide my cock into the hole and hope the woman on the other side is ready for me. The sooner this is over, the better. I don't enjoy my time in the club but after a while my hand and imagination just aren't enough anymore. I need human connection. But once it's over and the tension is gone, I can't help but feel dirty. I deserve the shame for what I'm doing, but it's never enough to stop me.

A soft hand wraps around my dick and I imagine it's Samantha's hand with the bright blue nails she's been sporting. The grip is firm but not too tight. I'm immediately fully hard.

I brace my hands against the wall as lips close over my head with a gentle suck. My eyes shut and I picture Samantha's plush mouth and bright red lips. The way her smile is somewhat crooked. The way she bites her top lip when she's focusing on a task.

The woman on the other side slides down my cock and holds the head at the back of her throat. She doesn't seem to be struggling, but I wait and hold my body rigid as I fight the urge to thrust.

At last, with a quiet moan, she pushes forward until I can slide into her throat. The tight, wet heat of her mouth driving pleasure up my cock and through my body.

"That's right, baby." I drop my head onto the wall and thrust my hips in slow, short movements. Her fist holds me where she wants me, giving me the freedom to move without worrying about hurting her.

As much as I resent this woman for not being who I want, I need her. And I don't want to hurt her. So, I close my eyes and imagine Samantha while I fuck the throat of some anonymous woman and hate myself for being so weak.

CHAPTER 4
JOSH

The cock slides in and out of me. His movements are slow, but I know that won't last. The type of man who comes to a glory hole isn't the type of man to show a lot of gentleness and restraint. They're here to get off, and they don't usually care if anyone else does.

Not that I ever get off. The witch that cursed me made sure I will never find release. She wants me to know the pain of edging and ruined orgasms. And oh, do I know it. It is my constant companion. No matter how many times or ways I thrust my aching cock against the inner wall of my prison, I cannot find relief.

The man behind me picks up speed, forcing himself into me harder and faster as he groans and mutters praise to the woman in front of me as she swallows down his dick. His dick, but not mine.

The witch's curse is as brilliant as it is cruel. The partition of the glory hole is my prison, forced to bear witness to endless pleasure but never experience my own release. I can hear the wet sounds, the sighs and groans. I understand the dirty words and damning prayers. But the pleasure is not mine.

A part of me has disconnected from my body. There is no hunger or exhaustion. I do not ache from being trapped, nor do I require sleep, though I am capable of it. I am just stuck, trapped in darkness and the sounds of the rooms around me.

That is, until the glory hole is in use. Which is where the real torment of the curse becomes clear. Trapped in the partition, I feel squished between two boards. They're a steady pressure on my body. All but my ass. Whenever something is pushed into the glory hole from the presenting room, I can feel it as though it's being inserted into me.

At first, it was all agony. My virgin ass hadn't been able to take the steady flow of cocks and straps presented through the wall. But now it's a different kind of pain. As the man drives his cock through the hole into the woman's mouth, I can feel it move inside of me. But while he can feel her warm mouth, my cock feels like it's being smashed between my pelvis and the wall in front of me.

And as the pleasure builds and pools inside of me, my cock rubs against the wall. It's hard and leaking, an endless pressure and ache. But no matter how deep they press or how much I thrust against the hard surface, there is no release for me.

"Oh, fuck." The man groans, and his hands ball into fists against me. One fist bangs against the wall and I can sense the woman jump.

I wonder if they're a couple who like playing dirty games. But I don't think so. Even though it can't be a coincidence that she's only ever in that room when he's there. She only takes his cock and then she leaves before anyone else can come in. But they don't move together like a couple familiar with each other. They don't talk through the wall like those couples do. There is no checking in or aftercare. He comes in, fucks her throat, and then leaves. And while he might talk dirty while his cock is buried inside of us, she doesn't make a sound.

I wish I knew what their dynamic is. It has to be a fascinating tale.

CHAPTER 5
SAMANTHA

push my underwear aside and slide two fingers inside my aching vagina. I'm so wet they slide in easily. My thumb finds my clit and presses as I continue to swallow down Harvey's hard cock.

This is so wrong. I know it's wrong. I'm deceiving him. I'm taking advantage of his weakness and my connections to make sure I'm the only face he fucks. He doesn't want this with me and my obsession with him is making it impossible to do the right thing.

But I shove that aside as I continue to swallow his cock. He's getting close. His movements are losing their steady pace and he's starting to go deeper and harder. I can hardly keep up with him, but I'm determined to take everything he can give me.

I pretend it's his fingers filling me as I fuck myself as best as I can while I suck him off. I pretend the stream of dirty words are just for me and not the random woman he thinks is taking him.

Does he know it's the same person as last time? Can he tell I'm the one who has been swallowing him down for the last six months? Probably not. I try not to let it hurt me.

I knew what I was doing the first time I saw the club's name on his agenda and made the choice to go. I knew it would end in pain after the first time I arranged with my friend, the club's manager, to be the one to take his cock. There is no way for us to move forward and there is no going back after I know the feeling of him on my tongue.

His groan carries through the wall as he thrust deep. I swallow his cock as deep as I can. Resenting the condom, keeping me from feeling his cum shoot down my throat. I want to taste him.

Finally, I have to slide off his cock or risk passing out from lack of oxygen. I keep my hand gripped around his base. This is the last time, I tell myself as I think about sliding the condom off and licking him clean.

He would never allow it, though. I know enough about Harvey to know he would leave in a moment and report me. Sanitation and safety are important to him in his work and I have no doubt it carries over to his play time. I can't risk causing a scene in the club.

I can't risk him finding out who is on the other side of the wall.

CHAPTER 6
JOSH

ow comes the flood of shame and quick retreat. It's a cycle I've experienced between these two for months and I can't take it anymore.

"Oh for fuck's sake, get over yourselves and get it together. I've helped a lot of people fuck but none of them fit together the way you two do."

The moment the words leave me, I wish I could take them back. These people aren't my witch, they don't know about my curse. There's no way this doesn't end horribly.

"What the fuck?" The man jerks out of me, it leaves me feeling hollow and aching.

"The fuck?" The woman echoes.

I listen as the man zips his pants and the woman scrambles into her clothes.

"Who's fucking here?" The man is pissed. Can't say I blame him. I'd be pissed too if I thought someone was peeping in on me having sex. Well, if they hadn't asked first.

Well, in for a penny, in for a pound.

"That would be me. The hole you were just fucking." I'd wave my hand if I had one. It just felt like a moment to wave. "Don't worry, I can't see you. It's not allowed."

"Whoever you are, you need to come out right now." The woman's voice is low and annoyed. The man stops moving around from where he was examining the corners of the room. I assume he was looking for a camera or speaker. Things he won't find. It's just the three of us.

"Say that again," the man demands, his voice low and brimming with danger.

The woman is silent. For a moment I wonder if she has sneaked out of the room, but then she shifts and I focus in on her rapid breathing.

Oh, this is interesting.

"Look, I'm just a hole in the wall, what do I know? But y'all have been doing this dance for months and seem to like it. Maybe get together without the wall between you and see how that goes."

The man hums low in his throat. The woman gasps and I hear fear there.

Very interesting indeed.

Fingers enter my hole from the man's side and I try not to make a sound. I'm so sensitive after the fucking I just received. The fingers circle my hole, looking for wires maybe? I'm not entirely sure what he expects to find.

"Are there speakers on your side?" He asks, still running his fingers along my hole.

"Nothing." The woman's voice is pitched low. She clearly knows him and doesn't want him to identify her.

"Maybe you should check for yourself," I encourage the man. I want to see what happens when these two come face to face. The intensity between them sizzles through the room.

"Maybe I should." The man withdrawals his fingers from the hole and I sigh in relief.

"No!" The woman's denial is nearly a shriek. "No, there's nothing."

CHAPTER 7
HARVEY

t can't be her. It has to be my imagination running away with me. It always did when I came here to try to get over her. I almost swore I could smell her green apple shampoo.

That fucking apple shampoo.

I am out the door of my room and around the other side of the booth in a flash. I am breaking every rule of the club and I could have my membership revoked. I don't care. I have to know.

The door is locked when I get there and I think about breaking it down.

"Open the door," I demand. There's silence from the other side. It goes on for so long I think she isn't going to obey, but then I hear the slide of the bolt. It barely stops before I push open the door.

There she is. For a moment I am certain I'm still imagining it because I want it to be her so badly. But she's standing there in the same tease of a dress she wore to work that morning and those sky high heels that have to kill her but she seems to prefer.

"I am so sorry. I know there isn't an excuse good enough for this. You don't have to fire me. I'll go pack up my stuff now and be gone by tomorrow."

The words are a stuttering rapids. Her eyes are wide and I can see her fear.

I have questions. So many questions. But none of them matter at the moment. The woman of my dreams just swallowed my cock, and I hadn't known. And now she was threatening to leave me. It was untenable.

Stepping into the room, I slam the door behind me and stalk forward. Samantha takes a small step back, but I don't stop. I'm done holding myself back when it comes to this woman.

"You're not going anywhere." I say just before I wrap my arms around her waist and drag her to me. She lets out a gasp, but that's all she has time for before my mouth crashes over hers in a searing kiss.

I've spent hours imagining what this woman tastes like, and I hate that my first sample was tainted with the taste of latex. But underneath, oh, underneath there is the taste of cinnamon and coffee. Things I will never be able to consume again without thinking of this moment.

Samantha's arms come up and I prepare for her to shove me away. Instead, her hands fist in my hair as she pulls me closer. At her permission, the last of my control snaps.

I slide my hands down from her waist to cup her ass and haul her up against me. Despite coming just moments ago, I'm hard again. In her heels, Samantha is about my height, which makes it easy to press my throbbing cock against the junction of her thighs.

My hands find the zipper of her dress and begin sliding it down.

"Tell me no," I murmur against her mouth. "Tell me to stop."

"Don't you dare."

CHAPTER 8
SAMANTHA

can't believe this is happening.

I fumble with Harvey's belt while he slides the zipper down my dress. It doesn't feel real, even as his lips slide down my neck and across the swells of my breasts. He mutters something into my cleavage I don't catch over my panting breaths.

The zipper releases, and Havey's hands come up to tangle in my hair. He yanks my head back until my eyes meet his.

"If we do this, you're mine." His words are a dark promise that sends shivers through my body. "We're going to talk about how you ended up here, but right now I don't care. I've wanted this for too long to wait."

I nod and mutter my agreement. It's enough to unlock him. His mouth comes back to mine and his hands slide my dress down my body to pool on the floor. I try not to think about the cleanliness of my favorite dress on the floor of a glory hole, even one in an upscale club. The growing distress floats away when Harvey reaches behind me to unclasp my bra and pull the lace garment away.

His head bends to my breast and I bow back to give him better access. I'm tall for a woman and

Harvey is on the short side for a man, putting us at equal height when I'm in heels. That equality makes the position pretty comfortable and Harvey seems to settle in, to lick, suck, and nuzzle at my breasts.

One hand braces my back as he holds me to him, as though I'm going anywhere. My hands fist in his hair, keeping him in place. His other hand skims down my body. The fingers tease my waistband before going lower to brush against my lips through the lace fabric. I shudder at the gentle contact.

"So sensitive," Harvey says, blowing a stream of warm air over my peaked nipple. "So sweet."

He rises to his full height and releases me. I nearly whine in protest. I need his hands on me. His mouth. I need him with a visceral intensity I've never felt before, and I doubt I'll ever feel again.

"When's the last time you were tested?" His eyes bore into mine as he slowly unbuttons his shirt. The slate tie he was wearing earlier is gone, but he's still wearing the rest of his suit. His jacket rumpled from my hands fisting the lapels earlier during our kiss. His belt is undone, and his shirt is half out of his slacks. Seeing Harvey, someone who prides himself on control and appearances, so un-kept is enough to drive me insane.

"Samantha!" He snaps his fingers at me and I flick my gaze up to lock on his. "When was the last time you were tested?"

"I had a physical just before I started working for you. I'm clean. And I have an IUD." Not be-cause I was sexually active, I haven't been in a long time. The IUD just helped make my periods toler-able without major hormonal shifts.

"Other partners?" His voice and eyes are dark. I

like the fact he's clearly put out by the idea of me with someone else.

"No one. You?"

There haven't been dates on his calendar but he could keep a personal one I don't see. Plus, he's been fucking a glory hole so who could say what else he gets up to.

"I haven't been able to see anyone but you in months." He shrugs out of his shirt and I take in the soft, muscular body. He's not firm and defined like a model, but he's trim and fit and I want to lick the trail of hair that leads from his belly button and disappears into his pants. I want to run my fingers through the mat of it on his chest. I want to lick the flat disks of his nipples.

I consider his words and want to ask him why he's here. Why, if I'm all he sees, he's so willing to fuck an anonymous mouth at a sex club. But I keep my mouth shut because I don't want to say or do anything that risks me, finally, getting what I want.

CHAPTER 9
HARVEY

consider the room as I shrug out of my jacket and shirt. It's sparse, nothing but the four close walls and the single rickety chair. If I had been capable of thinking, I would have dragged Samantha out of the glory hole booth and into one of the private rooms with actual furniture.

It is too late now. She stands there in nothing but her stilts and a scrap of lace underwear. There is no power on Earth that will convince me to let her get dressed before I have a chance to sink inside of her.

I toss my clothing over the chair and release the button on my pants.

"Strip." The word is a command and Samantha leaps to obey. She wiggles the scrap of lace down her legs.

"I'm not standing on this floor barefoot. I draw the line there." I can't help but laugh. I love her no-nonsense, no-arguments tone. I will have her obedience, but I am man enough to admit I love her fire. I had no desire to put it out.

"That's fair." I eye the dark tile floor that could conceal all kinds of fluids. I sure as fuck wouldn't stand barefoot on it. "Turn around, hands on the wall."

She barely pauses before turning around and pressing her upper body against the wall. Her back arches, her ass presented to me, a juicy offering ripe for my use. I close the short distance between us as I undo my zipper and slide my slacks and underwear down enough to free my erection.

I can see Samantha's pussy. It's already glistening in the dim light. I run a finger along the seam and appreciate the soft, damp flesh.

"So wet for me already," I slide a finger inside of her channel. She's so tight. Samantha gasps when I pull it out and return with a second finger. Preparing her for me.

"Yes, for you. Just you." She grinds her hips back on my hand as I slowly pump and curl my fingers inside of her.

"Did you fuck yourself while you sucked me off?" I ask her, twisting my fingers until I can press down against the bottom of her opening. She gasps and her pussy clamps down. "Did it get you hot having an anonymous cock in your mouth?"

She shifts to look over her shoulder at me. Her dark eyes are hazy but serious. "It wasn't anonymous. I knew who I was in here with."

I rock back on my heels as I consider the words. It shouldn't have been possible. Not with how the club works. But she sounds so confident in knowing.

"How?"

"Let a girl have her secrets." Samantha pushes against the wall until she's upright. She arches back until she can wrap an arm around my neck and pull me in for a kiss. "Only one of us was fucking strange tonight and it wasn't me."

I think about that and decide to let it drop. I

won't ruin the mood by explaining I was fucking a hole to get some relief from constantly wanting to fuck her. I knew enough about women to know it wouldn't win me any points.

I pull my fingers free from her body and bring them to my mouth to taste her. The musky taste explodes on my tongue. I groan around my fingers.

"You taste fantastic. One of these days I'm going to spread you on my desk and devour this pussy for hours."

"Later, fuck me now." Samantha arches again, pressing her ass against my bare, hard cock.

"Keep demanding and I'll make you wait until we get to my house." I slap her ass before gripping my cock to line up with her opening.

There was no way I would make her wait. I wasn't capable of waiting. I have wanted this too much for too long. There was no stopping us now.

"Please, Harvey, please fuck me."

CHAPTER 10
SAMANTHA

ince you asked so nicely."

I release Harvey and slap my hands to the wall as he eases his cock inside of me. He's so broad that it takes a moment for my vagina to respond to the stretch. It's almost painful, but he goes slow, easing his way inside of me.

Holy. Fucking. Shit.

Harvey Arivaca's cock is working its way inside of me. The reality of the situation tries to hit, but I don't let it. I won't let reality ruin what might be my only time with the man of my dreams.

It isn't just because he is an attractive, successful businessman. Those things don't hurt, but it's more than that. It's knowing how generous he is. How hard he works to make sure he can pay his employees a living wage with solid benefits so they aren't struggling to survive. It's how he always treats me as though I'm his equal more than his assistant.

Okay, maybe that last one is because he wanted to fuck me. But how was I supposed to know that? He never gave me any hint he was interested in me.

I clear my mind and focus on the feeling of Harvey's cock making its way into me. I am already so impossibly full and he is still driving forward.

When the tip of his presses against my cervix at the same time his hips connect with my ass, I can't help but moan. I've never been filled so fully or completely before.

"Fuck," Harvey moans in my ear, his breath hot against my neck. "You're the perfect fit. So tight."

He doesn't thrust. Instead, he starts a slow grind against my ass. It presses against my cervix, and the mixture of pleasure and pain is just right. One of Harvey's hands slides down to stroke my clit. It's perfect. Overwhelming. Amazing.

He continues that slow grind and pressure on my clit until I'm sobbing into the wall. My nails dig into the soundproofing panels and I squirm to get away from the overwhelming sensation.

"That's it, baby. Come on my cock." Harvey punctuates the words with a bite at the sensitive curve of my neck and I'm done. Gone.

I'm still flying high when Harvey's hands move to grip my hips and he starts moving in earnest. His hips slam into mine in a hard, punishing pace that has me pressed against the wall and doing my best to just hold on.

Over my steady stream of moans, I can hear him talking to me. It's a steady stream of praise and dirty words that has my head spinning even as my body is clenching around him. I'm riding the edge of another orgasm when he thrusts deep.

"Fuck, yes, come for me, Samantha. I want to feel you coming on my cock again." I don't even think about it. One orgasm rolls into the next until I'm nothing but a panting, whining mess.

"Yes, baby. That's it." Harvey gives a few short thrusts before he buries himself as deep as he can again and lets out a deep groan as I feel him spasm inside of me. Each hot spurt of his cum paints my walls.

He pins me to the wall with his body as we both catch our breath. My body is still shaking and covered in sweat, his cock still inside of me and I can't help wanting more. We both groan when he pulls out of me. A trail of his cum slides out after him and runs down my legs. His fingers swipe it up and push back inside of me.

"I like knowing you're going to walk through this club with my cum leaking out of you." His fingers thrust in varying depth with slow pumps and my already overly sensitive pussy throbs nearly painfully around them.

"You're coming home with me." He says the words as his fingers curl up to press against my g-spot. I whine and struggle away, but his arm bands around my middle and hold me in place.

"Yes, yes, whatever you want."

His fingers pull out of me and he brings them to my mouth. I open immediately, tasting both of us on his fingers.

"You're such a good girl. I can't wait to get you back to my bed and spend the night making you unravel."

CHAPTER 11
JOSH

listen as the couple cleans themselves up, muttering soft words to each other. There are kisses and sighs mingling with the rustle of material and zippers and buckles. If they make it home before fucking again, I'll be shocked.

Finally, they leave and I'm left alone again. The cleaning crew will come in soon and sanitize everything. Another pair will come to get off or get used. Whatever their kink is. The cycle will continue.

After the final check for the night, the door opens again behind me. I get the hint of citrus and sage, and I know who is there before she speaks.

"That was a nice thing you did. Very naughty of you to speak to strangers but a nice thing." Bethany strokes her hand down the wall, trailing her fingers along the hole but not pushing inside.

"I didn't mean for it to come out," I admit. Bethany's fingers circle my hole again and I try not to tense. Some days she's so gentle it causes an ache. Other times she's almost brutal in using me.

And it is about using me. She doesn't get off on it. Not sexually, anyway. No, her enjoyment is entirely based on my suffering.

I can't blame her. Not entirely. Not while I had

hurt her in the ways possible when we were together.

"I'll let it slide. This time. Samantha needed the push and she deserves to be happy." Bethany sighs and withdraws her fingers from the rim of my ass.

I tense, unsure if that means she is just going to tease me or if she is preparing to shove a giant dildo in my ass. It can go either way with her.

"Sweet dreams, Joshie." Bethany pulls away from me. "You have a busy day tomorrow. All booked up."

I'm left alone in the darkness again. That doesn't bother me, not anymore. But I don't know how to process the fact that Bethany did nothing but a soft tease.

For two years, she's taken great pleasure in my suffering. For two very long years she's fucked me, teased me, toyed with me until I am left begging for relief or release.

This was new, and I wasn't sure if I should be hopeful or concerned.

ABOUT THE AUTHOR

Sabrina Cross (she/her) is a neurospicy 80's baby from the middle of nowhere Michigan, where she still lives with her cat. She came into her monster romance era early when she fell in love with Beast from the 1997's X-Men animated series. After discovering sentient object romance in early 2023, Sabrina decided to embrace what she calls her 'Hold My Beer' style of writing and gave into the lifelong dream of being an author. When not writing weird monster/sentient object smut, Sabrina can be found hanging out on social media (@authorsabrinacross), reading, or hoarding office supplies.

ALSO BY SABRINA CROSS

Yarn & Monsters Series

A True Love Spell Gone Wrong...

When four friends perform a true love spell, things go terribly wrong. Now they're locked into a deal with the devil and have only a year to find love and happiness or their souls are destined to face the flames. Armed with a demon guardian; Clover, Jasmine, Fern, and Violet are determined to beat the devil and save themselves. Except, this curse might be the best thing that's ever happened to them.

Corny: A F/F Candy Corn Romance

A True Love Spell Gone Wrong…

A Demon Fairy Godmother?

Her very soul on the line. Can Clover still find true love or is she destined to face the flames alone?

Snuggle: A M/F Demon Teddy Bear Romance

A True Love Spell Gone Wrong…

Jasmine is too busy to go to Hell and she's definitely too busy for demon antics. But when her demon "Fairy Godmother" shows up, everything is on the line. Does she have what it takes to get out of the Devil's bargain or is she doomed to face the flames?

Tangled: A M/F Friends-To-Lovers Sentient Object Romance

A True Love Spell Gone Wrong…

Fern is going to Hell. Not metaphorical Hell but actual, physical Hell. But there's one thing she needs to do before she goes. An item she desperately needs to scratch off the bucket list. And she's hoping the demon sent to guard her will be willing to help her out.

Knotted: A M/F Demon Werewolf Romance

A True Love Spell Gone Wrong…

Violet was no witch but that didn't stop her from trying to use magic to find love. When the spell backfired and left her and her friends bound in a deal with the devil, Violet vowed to find a solution. Now, with less than two months until the deal comes due and zero leads, she's facing the fire. The fire comes early in the form of a great black beast in her bed. Does Violet find the love she's been looking for or does Hell claim her soul?

Light Me Up

He was the first man to ever turn me on. When he flipped my switch and lit me up that first time, I knew he was it for me. There would never be another.

Pounded by the Pommel Horse

Elena loves being on top. When the elite gymnast is challenged to defeat her gym rival on the pommel horse, she's up for the task. But is she up for the ride when the pommel horse shapeshifts into a man? A very, very naked Man?

Christmas with the Monster

He's Got a Package for Her… Devynn expected her first holiday without her kids to be difficult. But nothing could have prepared her for what she found under the tree just after midnight.With the help of his magic sack, the furry, green giant promises Devynn all kinds of pleasure. But would one night with the Christmas monster ever be enough?

Sentient Pen15 from Outer Space

Liam had spent a lot of his childhood obsessed with the legends of the local mines. The abandoned tunnels underground had driven dozens of workers insane and young Liam was desperate to get to the bottom of it. But he found more than he bargained for down there.

Infected by parasitic space mold, Liam has held himself away from relationships for years. When things spark between him and the girl next door, he has no choice but to reveal the truth: his manly appendage is also the bane of his existence.